THE BEARY DIFFERENT MAGNIFICENT BEAR

THE KINGDOMCUBS

We Bear The Good News!

Narrated By: Emunah La-Paz
Illustrations By Nadia Pro
Cover By Lavender Lashay

THE BEARY DIFFERENT MAGNIFICENT BEAR By:

Emunah La-Paz

illustrated By Nadia Pro

Narrator Audio Book: Actress Azell

Front Cover Lavender Lashay

Content Creator Malachi Hubbard

Copyright ©

2010 Publishers HSP

ISBN: 9780998275598

BEARY DIFFERENT MAGNIFICENT BEAR

TO: LAVY & MALACHI

IT's Okay To Be Beary Different!
www.thekingdomcubs.com

THE KINGDOMCUBS LLC.

We Bear The Good News!

Bearlinda always felt different
from all the other bears.
Bearlinda noticed that Bears in Bear
Kingdom, always seemed to stare.

Bearlinda was taller and bigger than all her friends. Bearlinda was even taller, than her art teacher Ms. Beary Fends.

Bearlinda often dreamed of having fur that was **deep** blue just like her friend Sue.

Sometimes Bearlinda wished

that she had simple fur, soft and brown,

like her friend Carmen

who always seemed to frown.

Bearlinda did not like her fur

of many c lors.

She wanted to look cool just

like the others.

Some of the other bears at school made

Bearlinda feel down.

They called her ugly and said that with her

fur, she looked like a clown.

Bearlinda was tall
and wished she were small, just
like her friend Paul, who was
good at kickball.

Bearlinda felt out of place. At times, she felt as if she took up way too much space.

Bearlinda's Mom said,
"Bearlinda, handle your fur with
care! Because you are,

The Beary Magnificent Bear!

Yet, Bearlinda, wanted to fit in not stand out! Bearlinda also notice that she had a very big snout!

Bearlinda's mom told her
that standing out is a good
thing a gift from above.
Bearlinda's mom said, "The color of your
fur, is A rainbow love."

Bearlinda noticed that her parents
were different just like her.
Her mom had patchy white and beige fur.

And her dad had sparkly jet-black fur that
he seemed to prefer.

Bearlinda often wondered
how two different bears
covered in different fur
could make a bear as colorful as her.

Bearlinda noticed that her friend Molly had parents that looked the same. Molly's parents had deep purple fur and Molly's fur was the same shade.

Her friend Dalia had parents with bright
yellow fur! Her Parents sparkled like
the sun; Just like her!

Bearlinda wondered why she looked so different it did not seem fair. Her mother smiled and said,

"Bearlinda, it's because you are,

The Beary Different Magnificent Bear! "

16

Bearlinda tried to roll in the mud to
change her fur brown.
Bearlinda's messy plan,
made her mom frown.

Bearlinda tried to dye her fur green, using green berries she found on a tree.

Bearlinda did not know that
she was allergic to green berries. She had
to stay home from school and listen to her
mom scold her about the toxic berries

Bearlinda tried to dye her fur red
like her friend Ted.
Bearlinda found some paint behind her
house stored in the shed.

But the paint was too sticky,
and a tad bit drippy.

The paint made a mess
throughout the house,
and this made Bearlinda's mom
shriek like an angry mouse!

"Bearlinda Mary Beary!
Your fur is all red!
Wash it off right now, and
go straight to bed!"

Bearlinda sighed and cried while she lay in bed. Yet to herself she thought, "Maybe tomorrow I'll dye my fur purple instead.

Bearlinda tried to talk her mom into dying her fur one solid color! Bearlinda wanted to fit in just like the others!

Bearlinda's mom said,

as she gently stroked her colorful

hair. "Berlinda! You are,

The Beary Different Magnificent Bear!"

26

"Your colorful fur was made

just for you!

I adore your fur!

And your dad loves it too!"

Bearlinda's mom told her not to worry or listen to negative
chatter. What is in her heart is the only thing that matters.
when Bearlinda Grew Older She no longer cared if the other bears
stared! Bearlinda grew up to be,

THE BEARY DIFFERENT MAGNIFICENT BEAR!

The End!

Collect All Of The
Kingdom Cubs.
Each Cub Represents Bearlinda's Emotions.
Each bear has their own obstacles to overcome

The Kingdom Cubs Series,
www. theKingdomcubs.com

Lightning Source UK Ltd.
Milton Keynes UK
UKHW050629170223
417164UK00028B/294